IN AND OUT THE WINDOWS

HARRIETTE CORET

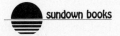
sundown books

New Readers Press • Syracuse, New York

This novel is a work of fiction. Names, characters, places, and incidents either are the products of the author's imagination or are used fictitiously, and any resemblance to actual persons, living or dead, events, or locales is entirely coincidental.

ISBN 0-88336-201-5

© 1982, 1990

New Readers Press

Publishing Division of Laubach Literacy International

Box 131, Syracuse, New York 13210

All rights reserved. No part of this book may be reproduced or transmitted in any form or by any means, electronic or mechanical, including photocopying, recording, or by any information storage and retrieval system, without permission in writing from the publisher.

Printed in the United States of America

Edited by Sharon Bywater

Illustrations by Sally Rubadeau

Cover design by Chris Steenwerth

Cover photo by David Revette

9 8 7 6 5 4 3 2

Chapter 1

Kit Ferris had been a girl much like other girls. But at 17, she changed. She had been a good student. Now, she could not study. She had been a lot of fun. Now, she became grim. She had had many friends. Now, she kept to herself. She had been secure and steady. Now, she was fearful. She did and said strange things.

One day, Kit's best friend, Rita, came up to her. Rita said, "Listen, Kit. My folks are going away for a few days. Do you want to stay with me while they are gone?"

Kit looked at Rita as if she had never seen her before. She stared at Rita's hair. At Rita's eyebrows. At Rita's rather big nose. Then she stared for a long while at Rita's teeth. "The better to eat me with," Kit mumbled. She turned and ran.

Rita yelled after her, "Kit! What's wrong with you? I thought you liked to stay overnight at my house."

Kit kept on running.

Kit was in trouble at home, too. One April evening she was in the front room. Her parents and sister were still at the kitchen table. She heard them talking about her.

"What has gotten into Kit?" Mr. Ferris asked. "She no more than sits down to dinner, then she gets up and leaves."

"I know," Mrs. Ferris said. "She acts awfully funny lately."

"She acts strange," Kit's sister Dee said. "I wonder if she is on drugs."

"Oh, no, not Kit," her mother said. "She's too straight for that."

"No one is too straight for that, Mom. Kids take drugs if their friends do."

"Sure," Dad said. "She's been seeing a lot of that fellow Russ. Maybe he put her on something."

"How do we find out?"

"We ask her. Give me a few minutes with her tonight." His voice sounded like her father's. But it struck Kit that this man was not her father. He was a secret agent sent to kill her.

How lucky she had overheard! If she hurried, she could save herself. She ran upstairs to her bedroom. She locked the door. She made sure the windows were locked also.

Kit saw herself in the mirror. She saw a tall girl with a healthy figure. Long, blond hair framed an oval face. Her features were regular. Her blue eyes were wide apart. The girl in the mirror looked flushed, as if she had a fever. "There is a book about that girl," Kit said to herself. "It's called *Alice in Wonderland.* I ought to read it to see what's going to happen to me next." The girl in the mirror smiled. Kit blew her a kiss.

The doorknob shook. "Let me in, honey." It was Kit's mother.

"Play it cool," Kit told herself. "Act as they expect you to act."

"I'm undressed," she called out. "What do you want?"

"Dee and I are going to the store for a few minutes. Dad will be here with you. When you get some clothes on, go down and keep him company. You hear?"

"I hear you."

"OK, honey. See you in a little while."

Kit put her ear to the door. She heard Dee ask, "Do you suppose she is shooting something into herself?"

"Shhhh," Mrs. Ferris said. Then the door closed. Kit knew she was alone in the house with a wicked man posing as her father.

She sat on the bedroom floor. Her back leaned on the door. She sat there for about 10 minutes. Then she heard footsteps on the stairs. The man was coming after her. What should she do? She slid toward the closet, opened the closet door, and slid in.

The man knocked on the door. "Kitty? Are you all right?" That proved that the man was not her father. No one had called her Kitty for years.

"Kit, if you are awake, answer me." He tried the knob. "I'd like to talk to you, Kit. May I come in?"

Kit's body froze. Would he force the door? No, he gave up. She heard him go downstairs again. A while later, she heard Dee and her mother come home. The closet was over the front hall. Kit found she could hear very well from there.

"She's asleep, I think," the man said.

"Well, then, let's leave it for tomorrow," Mrs. Ferris said. "The poor child might be tired. Some nights I feel like going to bed at seven myself."

Good! Kit came out of the closet. She opened a drawer of her dresser and pulled out a flashlight. Then she went back to the closet. She began to take pieces of paper from the pockets of her clothes.

Voices gave Kit messages. She wrote them down on little pieces of paper as she heard them. Then she hid them in her pockets—or in her shoes, or underwear. Every once in a while, she read them over. But she had not yet discovered their secret. This night, as she read, she felt sleepy.

She stuffed the papers into an old purse. Then she pulled a garment bag onto the floor. She crumpled up some dresses as a pillow. She crawled into the bag as if into a sleeping bag. Soon she was asleep.

When she awoke, it was light outside. She was getting dressed when she heard a car backing out of the garage. The man who called himself her father was driving off. Good! She could go downstairs without running into him.

She would go to school. Then, after school, she would run away. She would never come back to this house. She couldn't come back. It would be too dangerous.

Kit finished dressing. She went downstairs to the kitchen. "Hi," she said to her mother and Dee. She poured herself a cup of coffee and took two sweet rolls out of the oven. Dee smiled at her as she came to the table. Kit smiled back. "You look especially nice this morning," Kit said to Dee.

"Well, thank you. You look good, too. You must have slept well."

"I did. I slept especially well."

They sat and ate and talked together. Dee and Kit and their mother. Then Dee said, "Get your coat, Kit. I'll drop you at school on my way to work."

Mrs. Ferris's voice drifted out to the hall. "See, she's fine this morning. The poor thing was just worn out."

Dee drove in silence for a minute. Then she said, "Russ hasn't called you lately, has he?"

"Russ?"

"Yes. Your boyfriend. That's his name, isn't it?"

"Russy, fussy, cussy," Kit said.

"Is Russ on drugs, Kit?"

"Russer is a fusser and a cusser and a musser and a plusser and—"

"Kit, answer me! Did Russ put you on drugs? Are you taking something, Kit?"

"Russ is on drugs and mugs and hugs and lugs and—"

"Stop that, Kit! Tell me right out. Are you on drugs?" As she spoke, Dee drew up in front of school. Kit opened the car door. She got out and walked away. She did not close the door behind her.

* * *

A tall, thin, handsome boy stood beside Kit's locker. He shifted his weight and blushed as she came toward him. "Hello, Kit."

"Hello." Kit could not remember her locker combination. It didn't matter. The lock opened when she yanked it. She took out all the books that lay on the shelf. She started to close the door.

"Put your coat in," the boy said. He took her books from her. He put them on the floor and helped her out of her coat. Then he hung it in the locker. "You don't need all of those books this morning." He sorted out the books. He put some of them back and gave Kit the rest. Then he closed the locker door.

10

They started down the hall. "I need to talk to you," the boy said. "I want to know what's wrong. You know how much I love you. But lately, well, it's as if you don't know I'm alive. I'm scared to call you on the phone. You've hung up on me so many times. You won't look at me in class. Well, listen, I'm not made of stone, you know."

He looked sideways, trying to meet Kit's eyes. She looked away. "I'm beginning to think you're going out with somebody else," he said. "If you are, why don't you come right out and say so? You should say, 'I'm sorry. Russ, I don't like you anymore. I'm never going to marry you. Get lost.' Is that the way it is, Kit?"

Kit looked straight ahead. She said, "Russell gets muscles in his bustle when he hustles."

"Kit, I'm not in the mood for jokes. I'm worried about us, Kit. What's wrong with you? Have you gotten hold of some speed? Tell me, Kit, what is it? PCP? Who's feeding you drugs, Kit? Who are you going out with?"

Kit almost passed by Room 316, where she was due for first-period math. Russ put his hand on her arm and guided her in.

"Meet me by your locker after school," he said.

Ms. Hampton, the math teacher, was writing problems on the blackboard. Most of the class was copying them down. Kit took her math notebook. She turned to a clean page and started to copy the first problem. As she wrote, a voice said, "Go to the front of the room." She tore a piece of paper from her notebook. She wrote on it, "Go to the front of the room."

"Do it," the voice said. She wrote "Do it" on the paper. Then she put the paper in her pocket. She took her notebook and pencil. She slipped out of her seat and went to the blackboard. She stood there a minute.

"If you can't see from your desk, Kit, take one of these front seats. You are blocking your classmates' view," Ms. Hampton told her.

"Yeah, Kit, you'd make a better door than a window," Russ said, laughing.

Kit sat down in a front seat. She wrote in her book, "You would make a better door than a window." A lovely voice began singing the verses to a game Kit used to play in grade school.

Go in and out the windows.
Go in and out the windows.
Go in and out the windows.
As we have done before.
Go forth and choose a partner.
Go forth and—

Kit wrote the words she heard. There are many verses to that song. The voice sang one after the other. Kit wrote and wrote.

All of a sudden, Kit felt somebody near her. She looked up, startled. Ms. Hampton stood in front of Kit's desk. Kit looked around. The other students were gone.

"Didn't you hear the bell, Kit? Class is over."

"Oh." Kit started to gather up her things.

"Why did you write all through class, Kit?" Ms. Hampton reached out as if to look at Kit's notebook. Kit snatched up the notebook and stood up.

"You will see this over my dead body," she said.

"I don't mean to spy on you, dear. Is something wrong? I'm here every morning long before nine. Come in, and we'll talk about it."

Students were coming in for second period. Kit walked out of the room. She knew she could never come back to math class again. Ms. Hampton was part of the plot to kill her. Perhaps it would be better if she never came back to school at all.

She walked between rows of lockers. She felt confused. There was something important she must figure out. Let's see, Russ had wanted her to be a door. But the voice sang about going in and out windows.

Of course! That was a message meant to save her! Kit must leave school, not by a door, but by a window. But which one?

She looked around. She was in the hall by herself. Second period had started. There was no window opening out from the hall. Maybe in the girls' bathroom. She pushed open the door. No, the windows were way up high. She could never reach them, even standing on a chair. She came out.

Beside the bathroom was a door she had not noticed before. She was sure it was not a classroom. She tried the knob. The door opened. Kit looked into a narrow janitor's closet. A great big sink. A couple of floor-washing machines. Lots of rags and bottles of cleaner. Cans and sponges and mops and brooms. And, at the end, a double-hung window about two feet off the floor.

Kit went in. She closed the door and put her books down on a huge can that said Paste Wax. Then she went to the window.

The lock between the two panes was stuck. She struggled with it until her hands were sore. What might help? She looked around. Yes, there on a shelf was an oilcan. She stood on tiptoe and got it down. Sure! All the darn lock needed was some oil. It snapped open. Kit grabbed the handles of the window's lower pane.

Ugh! Had no one ever opened it before? She had to lift with all her strength. One inch. Two. Three. Then, with a great surrender, the window flew open the rest of the way. Plenty of room to go through!

Kit leaned out. She was two floors above the service entrance at the back of the school. Some trucks were parked there. A huge garbage box was beneath her. The rest was asphalt paving.

She rested one buttock and thigh on the sill and leaned out. How was she going to get down? It was too far to jump. That garbage box had handles and rough edges. It could hurt her if she hit it. There must be a way. The voice would not make her hurt herself.

Of course! How simple! On either side of the window, ivy spread over the bricks. The school was the oldest in the city. That ivy had been growing for fifty years, at least. It seemed to be stuck on the walls with heavy vine stems like ropes. All Kit had to do was put her feet over the sill. Then she could grab the ivy and let herself down on it.

A door slammed below her. A bald man with a big belly walked to a dairy truck. The man got in. He started the motor and began to back away. Then the truck stopped. The man got out.

"Hey!" he yelled up at Kit. "What the hell do you think you're doing up there?"

Kit's heart missed a beat. Oh my gosh, she thought. That fool will alert the whole school. They'll come after me. I won't be able to escape.

She got out of the window and ran to the closet door. No inside lock! She pushed the can of paste wax up against the door. Then she knocked down brooms and mops. She put the floor-washing machines into the narrow space between the shelves. It would take time to get through that mess.

She hopped back onto the window sill. The man was still outside his truck. As soon as he saw her, he started yelling. First to Kit. "Get in, I say!" Then to anyone who would listen. "There's a girl gonna jump out a third-floor window! Get her from inside!"

A couple of boys showed up from nowhere. "We'll call 911," one of them yelled. People seemed to spring up from the pavement. There were the school cooks and passersby, school children, teachers, workmen, neighbors. Now Kit heard the doorknob turn behind her. A man's voice said, "Oh, my God! She's blocked the door. Is there another way in?"

Kit reached out a hand and a foot toward the ivy on her left. "Ohhhhhh," the crowd below moaned. They started to give her advice. "No, don't move!" "Stay where you are!" "Get back inside!" "Wait for the firemen!"

Their orders came thick and fast. Kit couldn't sort them out. She brought her hand and foot back to the sill. She could see it would be hard for her to transfer her weight from the sill to the vines. She just sat there for a minute.

Then everything began to happen at once. Kit heard sirens coming closer and closer. She heard the can of wax slide on the floor behind her. She looked back over her shoulder. Mr. Frische, the principal, was inside the closet. He was picking up brooms and mops as he came toward her. A hook and ladder truck stopped below. "Go on!" a voice told her.

Kit swung her foot to the left. It came to rest on a little ledge. Of course! She remembered. The bricks of the building formed a design. Some bricks jutted out lengthwise. She had, by luck, found a brick sticking out. That gave her courage.

She grabbed the ivy with her left hand as she threw her body toward the building. She clutched at the ivy with her right hand. The leaves she grabbed came off the wall. Her right foot touched the wall. It found no support.

"Kit 'n' kaboodle! You've got holes in your noodle!" a voice said above all the screams from below. Kit screamed, too. The ivy in her left hand was coming loose from the wall. She was falling backward.

"It's all right. I've got you," a low, calm voice said. "Clasp your hands around my neck. Easy does it." A fireman was holding her around the waist. She was holding onto the side of his ladder.

* * *

Kit was still as the fireman carried her down. When he stepped off the ladder, she pushed at him. "Just a little way more," he said.

Everyone was staring at Kit. Some were laughing. Kit knew they were making fun of her. She didn't recognize any of the faces. Then she saw Rita. Rita had both her hands over her mouth. That girl doesn't want to bite me still? Kit thought.

Kit pushed against the fireman again. "Put me down."

"I'll put you down in that car," the fireman said. He nodded toward a police car. "They'll take you to a hospital."

"I don't need a hospital. I'm not hurt."

The fireman put Kit into the back seat of the car. A policeman was sitting there. "Help me! Help me!" Kit shouted. "These men are not policemen. They are going to kill me. They are secret agents."

A policeman opened the door by the driver's seat. He slid in. "I guess State's the best place," he said.

"Unless her parents want her someplace else. The school is getting them on the telephone."

Kit made a quick move for the door. The policeman grabbed her. "You don't want to do that. Come on. Relax. We're not going to hurt you."

Kit tried to hit him. But he held her arms so she couldn't. She tried to kick. But he said, "I'm not letting you out. I don't want to use handcuffs, so you'd better calm down. Let's go."

"Wait a minute. Here's someone now. There may be a message from her parents." Someone spoke to the driver. The driver said, "OK." The person opened the back door. He sat beside Kit. He closed the door. The driver started the car.

It was Russ. "Mr. Frische called your dad," Russ whispered. "He said to take you to St. Joseph's. I'll stay with you until your parents come. You don't have to be afraid." He patted her hand.

Kit didn't say anything to Russ. He didn't say anything more to her. He talked to the policemen all the way to the hospital. Part of the way, Kit sang, "Go in and out the windows."

Chapter 2

The Emergency Room at St. Joseph's was crowded.

"Sit down," the policeman said to Russ. "We have to wait for her father."

The policeman went to the desk. "We'll need a psychiatrist," he said. "Suicide attempt at Central High. Female, age seventeen." Then he sat down with Russ and Kit.

"I told you she was not making a suicide attempt," Russ said.

"How do you know?"

"I know Kit. You weren't trying to kill yourself. Were you, Kit?"

"There's that secret agent! There he is now!" Kit shouted. She pointed to the door. Her father was walking in. Kit jumped up and ran the other way.

"Whoa!" A big man grabbed Kit as she ran into him. "What's the matter here?"

"He's going to kill me." Kit pointed at her father. He was close to her now.

"Is this the girl from Central High?" the man asked.

"Yes. I'm her father," Mr. Ferris said.

"Why is she afraid of you?"

"Damned if I know! She was all right until today. Well, no, I take that back. She's been acting funny lately. Are you a doctor?"

"Yes. I'm Norton Waxman, a psychiatrist. I have offices here. They asked me to come down. What is your name?" he asked Kit.

Mr. Ferris answered instead of Kit. "Kathryn Ferris. We call her Kit. I'm Jim Ferris. Are you here to take care of Kit?"

"You are free to call in your own doctor."

"No. I wouldn't know who to call. May I speak to you, please?"

"Not yet. Let me talk to Kit first. You go into Admitting. Arrange for a bed."

"Listen, don't get the wrong idea. Kit's not crazy. She's just confused. She won't have to stay here. I'll wait for you, Kit."

"Don't let him hurt me," Kit begged Dr. Waxman. A voice said to Kit, "This man will save you."

"Paper! I need paper and pencil," Kit said.

"What do you need paper for?" her father asked.

"None of your business."

"I have paper in my office. Pencils, too."
Dr. Waxman offered Kit his arm. She took
it. They walked to the elevator. Kit held her
head high. It was nice to walk with Dr.
Waxman. She knew he would save her. The
voice had told her so.

Kit grabbed a pencil from a cup on Dr.
Waxman's desk. She tore a piece of paper
from a note pad and wrote, "This man will
save you." She folded the paper twice and
stuffed it into her shoe.

"Did you see those people?" she asked the
doctor.

"Sit down, Kit. What people?"

"Downstairs. Some were bleeding. Some
were black-and-blue. Some had to lie down."

"Yes. What about them, Kit?"

"Do you know why they were there?"

"Tell me."

Kit rose from the chair. She came close
to the doctor. She whispered, "They were
trying to save me."

"From what?"

"From the secret agents."

"I see."

"You could get hurt, too."

"I'll be careful." Dr. Waxman picked up
the telephone. "Admitting desk, please. Yes.

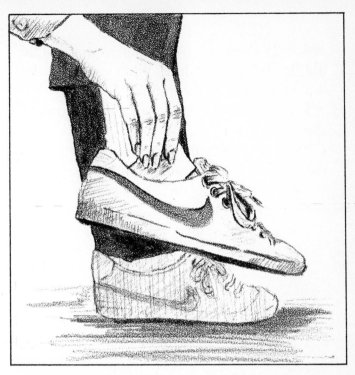

Hello. Has Mr. Ferris arranged for Kit to
stay?" he asked. "Yes. I think she should.
All right. Tell him to wait. I'll come down
and talk to him soon." He hung up. "Come
on, Kit," he said. "Your father said that you
may stay here for a while. Let me show you
where you'll be."

"I'll need paper and pencils."

"Sure," Dr. Waxman said. "Help yourself."

Kit took three pads of paper and half a
dozen pencils. Then she took hold of Dr.

27

Waxman's arm. A voice said, "Hey diddle diddle. Tell me a riddle. What's bald on the top? And thick in the middle?"

Kit laughed out loud. "Doctor Waxman," she said.

"Yes," Dr. Waxman said. He smiled even though he had not heard the joke.

"Will I see you again?" Kit asked him.

"If your father says so."

"He's not my father," Kit said.

Chapter 3

Kit stayed at St. Joseph's for two months. That was all the insurance her father had for her. Besides, she was much better by then.

For the first month, Kit drifted. Days came after each other like water flowing from a tap. They went down the drain. Kit could not tell one day from another. She took a lot of medicine. A nurse would hand her a pill and she would swallow it. Or a young doctor would give her a shot. She slept a lot. She sat in front of the television set. But she could not tell the story of what she watched. If a nurse or a patient spoke to her, she answered. She did not speak first.

Kit's parents came to see her. She did not say much to them. She did not look forward to their coming. She was not sad when they left. They were nervous. She was not.

On one visit, her father asked her, "Who am I?"

"What do you want me to say? A man named Jim Ferris? Mother's husband? My father?"

"That's what I want you to say, 'My father.'" Mr. Ferris leaned over and kissed Kit. There were tears in his eyes. Kit wondered why.

Russ came to see her, too. He brought her presents. The school newspaper. Her yearbook when that came out. Flowers. Cookies his mother baked. Funny cards.

Each time he came, he asked questions. How do you feel? When will you get out of here? Do you love me? Are they treating you all right? Is there anything you need?

Kit wanted to answer the questions. It was hard because she didn't know the answers. She didn't know how she felt. She didn't feel fine. She didn't feel bad. She mostly felt as if she were floating outside a body people called Kit. She didn't know how long she would stay in the hospital. She didn't care. She was glad to see Russ. She asked herself if that was love. She did not know. She did not much care about that, either. Most of the time she did not try to answer Russ.

"They have you so doped up, you act like a zombie," Russ stormed. "Tell them you won't take that stuff."

"All right," Kit said.

"You say, 'all right,' but will you really do it? Promise me you won't take any more drugs."

"It's medicine."

"That's what they call it. If a kid takes drugs, they put him in jail. But doctors shoot you full of the same stuff and call it medicine. Your folks pay them to put you on drugs."

"I have to take it."

Every time Russ came, he went home mad. Every time Russ left, Kit sat alone in the visitors' sunroom until bedtime. His visits upset her. Yet she wanted him to come.

* * *

Kit had a hospital roommate named Sally. Sally was 21 years old. She was depressed. Sally cried a lot. When she cried she would say, "Help me feel better, Kit." If Kit asked her, "What's the matter?" sometimes she would say, "Nothing." Sometimes she made many complaints. "I'm ugly. Nobody likes me. I hurt people. I never make the right choice. I don't feel well. I lose every job I get." The complaints went on and on.

Whatever Sally said, Kit always said, "That's too bad." Sally always said, "You don't care." It was true. The caring part of Kit was not working.

One morning, early in the second month, Kit was making her bed. Sally was in a good mood, for Sally. She was combing her hair a new way. She said to Kit, "We're sort of pals here, aren't we, Kit?"

A voice said to Kit, "Sally, Sally. She's your pally. Met her at a rally. Held in an alley. Held in a valley. Held in—"

Kit froze with the sheet halfway up the bed. One of those voices! She had not heard voices for weeks. She had forgotten about them. The voice frightened her. "Shut up!" she said out loud.

Sally looked away from the mirror. She held her steel comb high in her hand. "Don't tell me to shut up."

"I wasn't talking to you."

"There's nobody else here."

"People talk to me. I can't see them. But I hear them."

"Oh, ho! You have hallucinations! You are *really crazy*!"

"So are you."

Kit saw Sally coming toward her. "I meant, you're in the hospital, too. There must be something wrong with you, too."

Sally struck at Kit with her right hand. The comb she held raked across Kit's cheek. "Don't you dare call me crazy," Sally said. "You can't stand to see me have a good day, can you? You have to spoil it. If I'm not miserable, you have to make me that way. You're just like all the others. Just when I was starting to like you!"

A nurse, Ms. Martins, heard the fight. She ran into the room. "What goes on here?" she yelled. "Oh, Kit, honey! What happened to you?" Kit put her hand to her face. She felt something sticky. She looked at her hand. Blood was on her fingers.

"Oh my God! I didn't mean to hurt her!" Sally screamed.

Ms. Martins went to Kit. She tilted Kit's head back and studied her cheek. "I better send you down to Emergency," she said.

"How did it happen?" She went into the bathroom and got a smooth towel. She gave the towel to Kit. "Hold this to your face, dear," she said. "How did you get hurt, Kit?"

"I did it to her!" Sally shouted. "I didn't mean to! I'm so sorry! You'll never forgive me, Kit! I know you won't! You'll probably have scars the rest of your life! You won't be pretty anymore! How could I have done such a thing! Oh, I wish I were dead!"

"Hush," Ms. Martins said. "Go get Edna."

Sally seemed not to hear her. She threw herself onto her bed, sobbing wildly. "I hate myself. I hate myself. I wish I were dead!"

"Come with me," Ms. Martins told Kit. "Here, hold the towel like this. You don't want to rub with it."

They met Edna in the hall. Edna was a nurse's aide. She was delivering breakfasts to the rooms. "Here, I'll do that," Ms. Martins said. "You take Kit to the Emergency Room. Take her chart along. Give it to the doctor down there. Be sure he writes in it and gives it back."

* * *

The doctor in the Emergency Room was young and black. A bush of curls rose from his head. A beard and mustache almost covered his face. He looked at the chart for a minute. Then he took Kit into a small room. Edna came, too. An examining table, a sink, and a tiny desk almost filled the place.

"Sit up there," he said. Kit boosted herself onto the examining table. The doctor took the towel out of Kit's hand and guided her hand into her lap. He brought his face close to hers. She could feel his breath on her cheek.

"Oh, not too bad!" he said. "You know about dogs whose bark is worse than their bite? Yes? Well, this wound's bark is worse than its bite. It's just a scrape. I'm going to wash it off." He did so very gently. "Now, I'm going to put something on it to kill the germs. What caused the wound?" he asked Edna.

"I don't know," Edna said.

"It was a comb," Kit said.

The doctor looked at Kit with wide eyes.

"A comb!" he said. "Well, heaven knows what germs might lurk on that!" He picked up a cotton swab from a jar. He opened a bottle of clear liquid. He dipped the swab into it. Very gently, he painted Kit's cheek with the wet swab.

"Ow!" Kit cried out.

"Oh, it hurts, does it?"

"Yes."

"That's good," he said. He finished what he was doing, stood back, and looked at Kit. "Anyone ever tell you, you look like Alice in Wonderland?" he asked.

"No, but I used to think I did."

"You were right. You do. Need some help getting down from there?"

"No, I can do it." Kit jumped down.

The young doctor sat at the desk and wrote in Kit's chart. Then he gave it back to Edna.

"Don't eat any toadstools," he warned Kit. He had a nice smile.

* * *

Edna brought Kit back to her room. Sally was still on her bed, crying. When she heard Kit come in, she sat up. "Are you mad at me?" she asked.

"No," Kit said.

"Doctor Waxman wants to see you. He already saw me. Tell Edna to take your chart." Sally sighed. She lay down with her face in the pillow.

Edna knocked on Dr. Waxman's door. "Come in," he said. He rose from his chair and came around the desk. He took the chart from Edna. "Thank you," he said. "You don't have to wait, Edna. Come in, Kit. I'm sorry this happened. Sally is sorry, too." He looked at her cheek. Then he read the chart.

"Does your face hurt?" he asked.

"Yes."

"How does it hurt?"

"It—it stings."

Dr. Waxman smiled. "Sit down, Kit. Tell me, was anyone else in the Emergency Room?"

"Yes. Lots of people."

"Describe them to me."

"A little boy was crying. An old man was on a stretcher. There was a man with crutches, and—"

"What do you suppose happened to those people?"

"I don't know. Were they in accidents?"

"Maybe." Dr. Waxman smiled again. "Kit, Sally tells me this morning's ruckus started because you said, 'shut up' to a voice you heard. Is that right?"

"I think so."

"Do you hear voices often?"

"Not anymore. Before I came here, I heard them a lot."

"And you wrote down what they said. Did you write down what the voice said this morning?"

"No. Did I used to write down what the voices said? I don't remember doing that."

Dr. Waxman smiled again. He said, "Voices can persist after other symptoms leave. That is common. You have to learn to ignore them. Don't tell the voices to shut up. As you found out, that leads to trouble. Don't pay attention to the voices at all. Just give them the cold shoulder."

"Sally said I have hallucinations. She said, if you have those, you are really crazy. Am I crazy, Doctor Waxman?"

"Yes. But you're getting better, Kit. Hallucinations—hearing voices or seeing what's not there—are symptoms of an illness. A person with this illness seems to lose contact with the real world. We call the illness *schizophrenia*. There are other symptoms, as well. You have many of them, Kit. Therefore, we say you have schizophrenia."

"Will I always have it?"

"In a way, yes. The illness will always be there. But we are able to control it in some people. We can take away the symptoms."

"How?"

"With medicine. We don't understand how it works. It doesn't work on everybody. But with some people it works very well. You are one of those people. You are lucky. You responded right away."

"Sally told me I was crazy. So I told her she was, too. Is Sally crazy, too?"

"That depends on what you mean by crazy. Sally can't hold a job. She can't get along with people. She can't enjoy herself. She does sudden, mean things, like hitting you. If crazy means not getting along, then maybe Sally is crazy. On the other hand, Sally knows what is going on. She remembers well. She has no hallucinations and no delusions. She sees and hears what the rest of us do. She does not think people are plotting against her."

"Say that again."

"Say what again? That Sally does not think that people are plotting against her?"

"Yes. I thought that, didn't I?"

"Yes. Some schizophrenics think they are in danger. We call that *paranoia*. The first day you came here, you were in the Emergency Room. You saw people there. Do you remember?"

"Not really."

"Well, you thought they were banged up because they tried to save you. Today you supposed they were in accidents. Do you see the difference?"

"Yes. I do."

"You thought your father was part of the plot. He tells me you are no longer afraid of him. That's one way I know you're better."

"Am I better in other ways?"

"Yes. You said your face hurt when Doctor White treated it. Schizophrenics don't feel much when they are very sick. Hurting is a good sign. Another thing. You gave Doctor White a report of what happened. You remembered that Sally took a comb to your face. Most of all, we are sitting here, having this cozy conversation. We could not have talked this way a couple of weeks ago."

"Sally doesn't have schizophrenia, does she?"

"No. But schizophrenia is not the only mental illness. You and Sally both have chemical imbalances. That means something is wrong with your body's recipe. The chemical imbalance affects the brain. Different chemicals are out of whack in you and Sally. So you have different symptoms."

"Sally is not as sick as I am, is she?"

"Oh, I don't know. You were pretty out of it for a while. But your illness is passing. Poor Sally. She has been depressed for over a year. I have tried every medicine I know. Nothing seems to help. Depression is painful. Sally is worn out. That is why she is here. Schizophrenia is different from depression, just as mumps are different from measles. You find it hard to care, Kit. Sally cares too much. And," Dr. Waxman smiled, "doctors know too little."

* * *

Sally was still on her bed when Kit came back to the room. Her face was swollen from crying.

"Are they going to move you out of the room?" Sally asked.

"No one said so."

"I hope you won't go if they try it. I like you, Kit. I'm sorry for what I did. I'll make it up to you."

"It's all right," Kit said. "I'm not mad at you."

"You ought to be. I don't know how you can stand me."

"I shouldn't have said 'shut up' to the voice. And I shouldn't have said you're crazy."

"I said it to you first."

"But I am crazy. Even Doctor Waxman thinks so."

"So am I. Like you said, I wouldn't be here if I were normal."

"The way I understand it," Kit said. "I'm crazier than you are. But you suffer more."

Sally got off her bed. She put her arms around Kit. "You're the nicest person I ever met," she said. "Ms. Martins says your face will heal without scars. I'm glad. You'll be just as pretty as before."

* * *

Russ had a fit when he saw Kit's face. "Why do you let them abuse you?" he asked Kit.

"No one abuses me."

"You're all beaten up. Get out of here, Kit. This place is no good for you."

Mr. and Mrs. Ferris were shocked, too. "How could they put you in with a dangerous woman?"

"Sally isn't dangerous."

"She must be. Look what she did to you."

"It was a misunderstanding. She won't do it again."

"We will insist on a new roommate."

"No, Mom. I'll stay with Sally."

Chapter 4

One day Dr. Waxman said to Kit, "I think you should be in a group now."

"What do you mean?"

"Ms. Lloyd, the social worker, meets with some patients. They talk together. We call it group therapy. They try to help each other."

"With what?"

"With problems they may have when they go home."

"Am I going home?"

"In a matter of weeks. I'll tell Ms. Lloyd to call you next time her group meets."

Ms. Lloyd sent for Kit the next morning. She and five patients were in the sunroom. Ms. Lloyd put her arm around Kit's shoulders. "This is Kit Ferris," she told the others. "I've asked her to join us. Kit, this is Chris."

A tall man stood and shook Kit's hand.

"And this is Muriel."

"Hi," Muriel said. Ms. Lloyd brought Kit in front of a wicker arm chair. In it, a young woman sat curled up. Her face was half hidden in the chair's cushion.

"Karen, look here, dear. Kit is joining us." Karen did not turn her head. "You know what, Kit? Karen has a new baby at home. Maybe later she will show us his picture." Karen seemed not to hear. Ms. Lloyd guided Kit to the other side of the room.

"Here is Bert," she said.

Bert pointed to Kit's face. Then he said off to the side, "Did your old man catch you cheating on him?" He laughed as if he had said something very funny. He sat down and hit his leg again and again and again. "Your old man catch you cheating?" he repeated to the air. He laughed some more.

"And this is Janet," Ms. Lloyd said. "She's just your age. Ask Kit to sit by you, Janet."

"Sit down," Janet said. Kit sat in the empty chair next to Janet.

Ms. Lloyd sat down, too. "Janet, have you decided to live with your mother? Or with your father?"

"I told you, I won't live with either one. They made me sick. If I go back to them, I'll get sick again."

"Nobody can *make* you sick, Janet. Schizophrenia is an inherited tendency. Maybe the stress of your parents' divorce was bad for you. But it could not give you schizophrenia."

"Believe in the Lord," Chris said. "It doesn't matter where you live. Do you go to church, Kit?"

"Are you talking to me?" Kit asked.

"Yes. Do you go to church?"

"Sometimes."

"Janet, you change places with me," Chris said. "I have to talk to Kit."

"No, you stay put," Ms. Lloyd said. "We are all trying to help Janet. Janet has a problem. She can live with either her mother or her father. But she wants her own apartment. Is she ready for that? Kit, you are Janet's age. Are you going to live with your parents?"

"Yes," Kit said. "But I want to."

"See!" Janet shouted. "She wants to. I don't want to. Maybe her parents are nice. Mine aren't."

"Be careful!" Chris shook his finger at Janet. "Jesus said to honor our fathers and our mothers. God might strike you dead for what you said, Janet."

Jesus didn't say that, Kit reflected. That was one of the commandments God gave to Moses. But she did not correct Chris. She was a little afraid of Chris.

"Let's talk about what Chris just told Janet," Ms. Lloyd said. "How many of you think God will strike you dead if you think bad thoughts?" Only Chris raised his hand.

"Many young people find fault with their parents," Ms. Lloyd said to Chris. "Let's not scold Janet. She is telling us how she feels. Let's listen."

"Stop listening!" Janet shouted. "I'm getting my own apartment. That's that! You all give me a pain."

"If you're by yourself, you'll forget to take your medicine," Muriel said. "That's what happens to me. I lose track. I wish I had someone to go home to."

"You can live with me," Chris said.

"With you? You can't even take care of yourself."

"The Lord will take care of us both."

"Tell us, Muriel," Ms. Lloyd said. "How is it with you when you leave the hospital? You've been here before, haven't you?"

"Three times. When I go home, it's nice for a few days. Then there's too much and too little."

"Of what?"

"Of everything. Time. Sleep. Food. Things to do. Things to remember. People. Work."

"Can you describe that?"

"I sleep too much. Or not enough. I think the place is clean. Then, all of a sudden, it's so dirty I don't know where to begin. I buy too much food. Or not enough. Things never come out even. Then I lose track."

Kit thought of Dee. Even if her parents were dead she would still have Dee. "Maybe you can live with a sister," she said to Janet.

"If you knew my sisters," Janet snarled at Kit. "I'd rather be dead!"

Kit met with the group for an hour every day until she went home. It's funny, she thought to herself. I can see how each one of them could make things better for himself. Yet, I can't see what I should do. I seem to understand them. But I don't think they understand me. Is that because I'm sick? Or because they're sick? Or is that just the way it always is?

Chapter 5

On a pretty June day, Kit went home. Her parents picked her up. Her mother had an especially nice lunch waiting.

"Well," Mrs. Ferris said, "It's sure good to have our Kitty back again."

"It sure is," Kit's father said. "It's going to be like old times."

"That's right," her mother said. "Eat some celery, Kit. It's good for you."

"Since when do you eat whole wheat bread?" Kit asked.

"Since we started with the Huxley Institute," Mrs. Ferris said. "They think diet has to do with schizophrenia."

"I bake the bread myself," Mrs. Ferris said. "And we eat oatmeal for breakfast. We're off coffee. No sweets."

"Because of me?"

"Partly. It's good for all of us. Dee has lost three pounds."

"Did you ask Doctor Waxman?"

"Yes. He says it's fine. So long as you take your medicine," her father said.

"I'm convinced," Mrs. Ferris said. "We poisoned you with all that bleached flour."

Home was the same. Yet it was different. Kit's parents kept telling her what to do. "Come watch TV. You always liked that," they said.

"No. I don't feel like it."

"Why not, Kit? It will do you good to laugh."

Kit was not able to laugh at the TV shows. Her sense of humor was out to lunch. Besides, her mind wandered.

"Go take a walk," her mother said.

"All right."

"Change your slacks first. Those are too tight."

By the time she changed her slacks, Kit forgot about the walk. She stretched out on her bed.

Kit spent a lot of time in her room. That bothered her parents. They called her to come downstairs. "What do you do up there?" they asked.

"Nothing much," Kit answered.

That was true. In her room, Kit lay on her bed. Or looked out the window. Or tried to read. Sometimes she tried to figure out what happened to her. How did it begin? She found pieces of the answer. They frightened her.

The first day she was home, she wanted to change into something comfortable. She went into her closet. She took down a housecoat. She put it on. There was something in the pocket. She drew out a slip of paper. The paper said, *Little Jack Horner is a foreigner.* What in the world was a nutty sentence like that doing in her housecoat? Who put it there? Kit studied the paper.

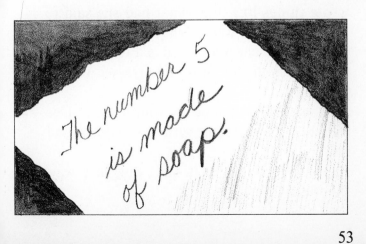

Whose handwriting was that? A chill came over her. It was her own.

Someone had brought her school things home. They were on her desk. She opened a notebook. There, along with her English notes, she found more weird messages. One said, *Black and Brown smell bad.* Another said, *The number 5 is made of soap.*

She opened her math notebook. There were all the verses of *Go In and Out the Windows.* Why that? She hadn't played that game since third grade. "What other crazy things have I done?" Kit asked herself.

She searched her room. She found many notes in an old purse. Each time she read one, her heart stopped for a second. The messages were so absurd! So stupid! If she wrote things like that, what had she said to people? What a weirdo she must have been! It was as if she had lived a life she knew nothing about. She was embarrassed to face people.

"You shouldn't hide in your room," Dee told her. "Come out with my friends and me."

"I'm not hiding," Kit said. But, in a way, she was.

* * *

A few days after Kit came home, Rita came to see her. Rita brought along a girl named Ellen. Rita and Ellen were going to play tennis. "Come with us," Rita said.

"I don't play tennis."

Ellen and Rita looked at each other. "Three can't play. We meant for you to watch us."

"No, thanks."

Rita seemed relieved. "Bye, Kit," she said. "I'm glad you're home. I'll call you." Then she let the cat out of the bag. "Bye, Mrs. Ferris. Thanks for telling me Kit is back."

"Well," Mrs. Ferris said. "It was nice of Rita to stop by. That Ellen seemed like a nice girl, too. Would you like to take tennis lessons? It would be good exercise. You could play with Rita."

"No," Kit said. "Only two can play tennis. Rita already has a partner." She hoped Rita would not call her.

Rita had graduated from high school. So had Russ. So had Kit. Central High School sent Kit's diploma in the mail. A letter came with it. The letter said that Kit should finish her courses at home. She could take as long as she wanted. Each teacher sent a note saying what to do. Write a paper. Or do some• pages of math. Or read a certain book. In the meantime, they let her graduate with her class. So she would never have to explain, they said.

"Isn't that nice?" Mrs. Ferris said to Kit. "You can be proud they trust you."

They are afraid I'll come back and upset things, Kit thought. She didn't feel she had graduated. She felt they had given her a diploma to get rid of her.

* * *

Russ came when he could. He had found a job at a lumberyard. The work was hard. The hours were long. But he earned good wages. He was also helping his father paint their house. He was not used to working like that. He was tired. Sometimes he was crabby.

"It will be different when we're married," he said. "Then I'll come home to you. I won't have to fit you in. You'll be there all the time."

"I'll like that," Kit said. "But let's wait. I'm not ready."

"You know how long I intend to wait? Just until your face loses those scabs. I don't want my bride to have comb marks on her face. But no longer."

"That's not fair," Kit said. "I don't feel good yet."

"That's because you are back in this house. Your parents treat you like a child. That's why you got sick. Your parents do your thinking for you."

"They do not. They give me lots of freedom."

"You *think* they do. They don't want you to grow up. They want you to be their little Kitty forever."

"You don't understand."

Kit and Russ had the same argument many times. Different words. Same fight.

Russ watched Kit in the same way her parents did. "You are getting fat," he said one night.

"I know that. Doctor Waxman says the medicine does it."

"Stop taking the medicine."

"I have to take it. I take vitamins, too."

"Vitamins! Too many vitamins can make you sick."

"How do you know?"

"Everybody knows that. They print it in the newspaper."

Russ and Kit had that fight over and over again, too.

Kit began to wonder if Dr. Waxman was a good doctor. She wondered if her parents knew what they were doing.

Chapter 6

August 15 was Kit's 18th birthday. Russ took her to a floating nightclub. She was all dressed up. So was he. The moon reflected on the river. The band played. The air was balmy. Other couples laughed and sang. Kit and Russ stood by the rail. Russ looked into Kit's face. "I love you so much," he said. "I hate to see you wasting your life. Let me help you."

Kit felt something she hadn't felt in a long time. She reached over and kissed Russ on the cheek. "Oh," she said. He put his arms around her. He hugged her. He kissed her lips.

"I love you," Kit said. "You are the best person I've ever known. I don't know what I would do without you. I love you. I do. I do."

"Then marry me soon. Oh, Kit! I need you so much! I make enough money to support us both. Please, Kit!"

"All right," Kit said.

"But you have to stop taking that medicine," Russ said. "It's doing bad things to you, Kit. You used to be fun. You liked to go out. You said funny things. You liked to be with people. Now, look at us. We're all by ourselves. You don't even want to dance. You have to get away from your folks. They are bad for you. Stop seeing that doctor. Be your old self." He kissed her again. "Well, I feel good," he said. "Let's go in and have a hamburger."

"I can't," Kit said. "I'll order a salad."

"See what I mean?" Russ grumbled. "You've got it in your head that you're sick. You're not sick, Kit. Stop taking that medicine. Get back to your old self. Quick!"

Kit lay awake most of the night. Maybe Russ was right. Maybe her parents did want to keep her a child.

She had seen Dr. Waxman only twice all summer. Each time he had said she was doing well. He had not talked much to her. He didn't care about her. Russ did care. Russ might be the only person who would ever care. On the boat, she had felt a great wave of love for Russ. That felt great! If she married Russ, maybe she'd always feel good like that. The medicine was making her fat and dull. Why take it?

In the morning, she did not take her medicine. She did not take it the next day. Nor the next. She did not take it all that week. Nor the next week. She felt good. Her spirits rose. She moved faster. She talked more. She went for walks. She had ideas.

One day she came home from a walk, bursting with joy. "I was down by the ice cream parlor," she told her mother. "A man was putting a sign in the window. It said Waitress Wanted. I went in. I said, 'I'm that waitress you want.' He said, 'Okay.' He hired me. I have a job!"

"I can't believe it!" Mrs. Ferris said. She hugged Kit. "You're getting well so fast. Doctor Waxman said you wouldn't be able to work for a while. He didn't know our Kit!"

"Oh, that Doctor Waxman! What does he know!"

Kit did not keep her next appointment with Dr. Waxman.

Chapter 7

Kit's first week at the ice cream parlor went fine. She gave people what they ordered. She packed cartons to take out. She brought home her first paycheck and took her family to the movies.

"See!" Russ said. "You're like a new person. You're even losing weight."

"You were right," she said. "You are always right. It is going to be wonderful being married to a man who is always right." She began to tickle Russ.

"Cut it out. You know I hate that."

Kit worked on Labor Day. Midmorning, the boss called her over.

"I'm missing three of these," he said. He pointed to a pile of order slips. "Are you handing them all in?"

Kit felt in her pocket. One order slip was there. Another was in her other pocket. Kit was about to hand them in with the money.

But, each time, a voice said something to her. She had to write down the message on the slip. Then she couldn't hand it in.

"I give you all the money," Kit said.

"I am not accusing you of stealing. I just want the slips. Hey! What's this?" He reached behind the band Kit wore around her hair. He pulled out a folded slip. He unfolded it. "What the devil!" he said. "*Two mocha-almond cones. One caramel sundae. One malt. Mocha, polka. Pudding and pie. All these desserts. Make a fat I.* What are you doing? Writing a musical on the order slips?"

"I didn't make that up. Somebody else did."

"Then what was it doing in your headband?"

Kit did not answer. She walked away.

The boss kept watching her. At noontime Kit served two women. One of them laid a package down beside her. Kit whispered to her, "Hide that package."

"Why?"

"I can't pick it up here. We'll have to meet outside."

"Whatever do you mean?"

Kit leaned very close to the woman. She whispered, "Your friend is a secret agent." She took their order and walked away.

The boss could not hear what Kit had said. But he saw the woman twirl her finger near her head. She and her friend laughed. After Kit brought their lunch, the one said to the other, "Do I dare eat it?"

"You mean, do *I* dare eat it," her friend answered. "After all, *I'm* the secret agent." They laughed again. The boss did hear that.

"When it slows down, come to my office," he told Kit.

"Ah ha!" Kit said to herself. "As if I didn't know he's an agent, too. He'll kill me in his office. I better get out of here."

The boss turned his back. The door was open. Kit made her getaway. The lady with the package was leaving at the same time. Kit almost knocked her down.

"That girl really is crazy," the woman said.

"It's disgusting," her friend answered. "They let them out too soon. They take jobs sane people could fill. It's really disgusting."

* * *

Kit walked all afternoon. Up one street. Down another. Voices spoke to her all the time. She answered them out loud. She almost got run over. She fell once. But she wasn't hurt. It was dark when she got home.

"Where have you been?" her mother shouted.

"Waiting tables."

"You still have your uniform on," Dee said. "How come you didn't change?"

"It needs washing," her mother said. "Put it into the hamper, Kit."

"All right." She went toward the stairs.

"Aren't you hungry?" her mother asked.

"No. I ate." Had she eaten? Kit could not remember. It was not important. The important thing was that she write down what the voices had said. She sat at her desk. She opened one of her school notebooks. She started writing. She wrote for hours. Then she slept in the garment bag in the closet.

When she awoke, she heard voices. Not hallucinations. Real voices. She looked out the window. Boys and girls were going to school. It was the first day of the new school year. They were excited.

Oh my gosh, she thought. I'll be late.

She went to her closet. She pulled out a skirt and blouse she had worn to school the year before. She put on low-heeled shoes. She took her notebooks from the desk. She ran downstairs and out the front door. She walked to the high school.

At school, she went to her last year's locker. She jerked open the lock. She put her English and science notebooks on the shelf. She kept the one for math. She went to Room 316. She sat at her old desk.

Ms. Hampton saw her. "Why, hello, Kit. I didn't know you were coming back." Ms. Hampton looked at a paper on her desk. "You're not on my list, Kit."

Kit stood up. "I'm not on *that* list. Look on your *hit* list, Ms. Hampton. Do you think I am going to sit here and wait for you to strike? I'm not! You'll never catch me."

The students tittered. "That's that crazy girl," one said.

"Oh, yeah! The one that went out the window."

Kit went into the hall. Ms. Hampton called after her.

Kit did not turn around. Ms. Hampton must have called the office. Mr. Frische met Kit in the hall.

"Hello, Kit," he said. He took her arm. "Let's go to my office."

"No. Let me go." Kit tried to free her arm.

"I called your father. He's coming."

Kit began hitting Mr. Frische. "Hal!" Mr. Frische called to a boy in a football sweater. "Take her other arm."

It was walk or be dragged. Kit walked to the office. Her father's face was white. He looked 80 years old.

"Oh, Kit," he said. "Not again."

Chapter 8

Kit was in St. Joseph's only two weeks this time. Big doses of medicine made her groggy at first. But she recovered fast. Dr. Waxman sent for her after a few days.

"I'm sorry to see you back so soon," he said. "You went off your medicine. Didn't you?"

"Yes."

"And you stopped coming to see me."

Kit looked at the pencil cup on Dr. Waxman's desk. She did not answer.

"You were doing so well, Kit. Didn't you realize that? I was going to reduce the medicine."

"I felt heavy. And dull. Like I do now. Russ, my boyfriend, got tired of me. I was boring."

"You want to please Russ?"

"Yes."

"How about your parents?"

"I want to please them, too. But Russ says they are not good for me. He says they baby me."

"What does Russ think of me?"

Kit bit her lip. She looked at her lap. "Russ is a good person," she said at last. "He means well."

"No doubt! But Kit, I'm a good person, too. Your parents are good people. We all mean well."

"Russ thinks doctors just want the money."

"Russ is wrong. You responded to my treatment. That made me feel good. Not all my patients improve. I feel bad when I don't succeed with them. Of course, I want to be paid for my work. But success means more than money."

"I'm sorry. I love Russ. I want to marry him. I was hurting him. Now I'm hurting my parents. My dad has to pay for me here. The insurance ran out. He has to draw out savings." Kit began to cry. "I guess I hurt you, too."

Dr. Waxman came around the desk. He gave Kit a tissue. He drew a chair close to Kit's. "You're crying," he said. "And you care. Those are good signs. You are getting better fast." He put a hand on her shoulder. "You're a good person, too. You mean well, too."

Kit wiped her eyes and her nose.

"Tell Russ to come see me on Tuesday at three. You come with him."

* * *

Russ was nervous about meeting Dr. Waxman. But he came.

"You don't understand," he told Dr. Waxman. "Kit's parents seem nice. But they don't let Kit breathe. They protect her too much. That's why Kit had a breakdown."

"You are the one who doesn't understand," Dr. Waxman said. "Kit has a tendency to schizophrenia. The tendency came into the world with her. She inherited certain genes. She did not have a breakdown. She had a flare-up of what was already there."

"But if her parents had been different—"

"Or if you had been different!" Dr. Waxman said.

"What do you mean?"

"Good things can be as stressful as bad. It is nice for a girl to have a boyfriend. But that boyfriend can become too serious too early. If the girl is not ready—"

"Is that right, Kit?" Russ asked her.

"I don't know, Russ. I can't think clearly for myself. So I rely too much on you and my folks. They expect one thing. You expect another. That tears me apart."

"You can't think clearly because you are doped up. The medicine is making you stupid."

"That's partly true," Dr. Waxman said. "When Kit is in a schizophrenic spell, her thoughts race all over the place. She can't control them. A big dose of medicine controls the racing. But she finds it hard to think. We will cut down the medicine. Then Kit will find a balance.

"You see, first we must give her a chemical wallop to get rid of the hallucinations and delusions. Then we reduce the medicine. We find a dose that gives her control. But one that lets her think. Some schizophrenics can give up the medicine in time. Some can't.

"Think of it this way, Russ. Kit is a beautiful hot-air balloon. She got caught in a storm. The storm threw her this way and that. Somehow we got her to earth. We tied her to the ground. When the weather is fine, we'll let her go up again."

"Where does that leave me? I love Kit. I want to marry her."

"That's fine. I hope you do marry her. But wait. Make sure there are no storms. Give her a chance to sail by herself for a while."

"Is it fair to Russ that I marry him?" Kit asked.

"Why not? A person with schizophrenia can have many spells. If Russ understands that, you are not fooling him."

"If she marries me, she won't get sick again. I'll be good to her. You'll see."

"No, Russ, it doesn't work that way. If you marry Kit, yes, be good to her. But she can get sick, anyway. If she does, it will not be your fault. Remember that."

"You said schizophrenia was in Kit's genes. Does that mean we should not have kids?"

"That's up to you. We don't know enough yet. I can't advise you not to have children. Nor to have them. Wait and see."

"The big word is W-A-I-T," Russ said.

"Yes," Dr. Waxman said.

"Maybe you don't want to wait, Russ. If not, I'll understand," Kit said.

"But I do want to wait," Russ said. "You're worth waiting for." He turned to the doctor. "May I kiss her, Doctor Waxman?"

"By all means. Be my guest."

Chapter 9

Russ's 19th birthday was November 8. Kit knitted him a red cap. And red mittens. And red socks. Mrs. Ferris invited Russ's family for dinner on that date. Kit helped her mother make a fancy dinner. Her sister, Dee, baked a birthday cake.

Russ opened Kit's present. He put on the cap. He wore it as he ate. Everyone was happy. They talked and laughed a lot. Dee brought in the cake. She said, "With this cake, I beg your pardon, Russ. I thought you put Kit on drugs. I was wrong. I'm sorry."

"That's all right," Russ said. "I had some funny ideas myself."

Russ blew out the candles. He cut into the cake. "Hey, this looks good. I thought you people didn't eat sweets anymore."

"Oh well, for a special occasion, a little won't hurt us," Kit's mother said.

"Good. I was afraid I might never have cake again."

"No one said you had to share the diet."

"But if Kit and I marry, I'll have to eat what she cooks."

"Never mind," Mrs. Ferris said. "Kit is a good cook."

"She is? Well, in that case, let me give myself the best present of all." Russ reached into his pocket. He pulled out a velvet box. He flipped up the lid. A diamond ring was in the box. "This is my present to me," he said. "But it also means you will marry me. Hold out your finger, Kit."

Kit held out the third finger of her left hand.

"I'll wait as long as you want me to," Russ said. He kissed Kit.

"I love the ring. I love you, too. Thank you." Kit kissed him back.

"We're glad the children decided to wait," Russ's father said. "We want Russ to take business courses. If he picks up skills, he can advance at the lumberyard."

"Yes," Russ's mother said. "Why don't you go with him, Kit? You do things well. If you don't want to study, take crafts."

"Yes," Russ said. "Let's enroll at the junior college second semester. They have evening courses. It doesn't cost much."

"I'll think about it," Kit said. "I hope to have a job by then." She knew she would do it. They trust me to get well, she thought. Russ's parents as well as my own. I am very lucky. They understand.

Later Russ's family went home. Kit and Russ went for a walk. Kit skipped a little and hummed a tune.

"I think the balloon is beginning to rise," Russ said.

"Oh, don't think of me as a balloon." Kit laughed. "I'm fat. But not *that* fat."

"Just nicely rounded," Russ said.

"Whatever! I don't like being a balloon. Let me tell you how I see me."

"Tell away."

"You know how on television they show oil slicks? A ship leaks oil. Or a drill gets loose. Oil spreads on the ocean. Sea birds land on the slick. They can't take off again. Their wings are coated.

"Kind people go out in boats. They grab the birds in nets. The birds fight to get away. The rescuers take the birds to land. They wash their wings. Then they shoo the birds back out to sea.

"The birds don't want to go. They are afraid. Besides, the washing takes natural oil out of their feathers. They can't fly as well as they used to. They feel funny.

"Schizophrenics are like that. They are sea birds. They land in the oil. Then they fight their rescuers. They don't want their wings washed. Yet it has to be done. Afterward, they are glad. But the washing takes away more than just the symptoms. It takes away some parts of the personality. It takes a while for the personality to be whole again."

"Do you see the medicine as the washing?"

"Yes. And being in the hospital. And being watched and told what to do."

"Maybe the sea birds should learn to live on land."

"No. They can't. They are what they are. They were born sea birds. They have that extra risk born in them."

"You're coming out of it, Kit."

"I know I am. Russ, when we go to college, I want to take a writing course. And some music. Some of the things my voices said were funny. I said those things myself. The voices were in my head. My boss at the ice cream parlor asked if I was writing a musical. Maybe I *can* write a musical comedy."

"Maybe you can," Russ said. He took her hand. He gave it a squeeze. Kit squeezed back.

What would be, would be. They had pledged themselves to each other. Now, hand in hand, they walked on together.